First published in Great Britain by HarperCollins Publishers Ltd in 2003

1 3 5 7 9 10 8 6 4 2

ISBN: 0 00 715306 6

Bang on the door character copyright:
© 2003 Bang on the Door all rights reserved.
bang on the door® is a trademark
Exclusive right to license by Santoro

www.bangonthedoor.com

Text © 2003 HarperCollins Publishers Ltd.

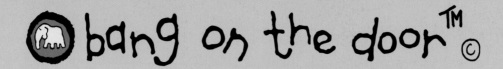

bang on the door™ ©

the cool sleepover secret

Collins

An imprint of HarperCollinsPublishers

Little sweetheart was having a sleepover. But she was sure she had forgotten something.

"What can it be?" she wondered.

Little tough guy was the first to arrive. "I'm going to stay up all night!" he said, swinging his sword.

"Ding-dong," went the doorbell.
It was **little tinker** carrying a very big bag.
"Is that a new laser sword?" asked **little tough guy**.
But **little tinker** wouldn't tell.

"It's a secret!" he said mysteriously.
With a flash of swishy purple cape, **super hero boy**
zoomed in waving his toothbrush.
"Oh, my!" cried **cutie**.

As soon as **little madam** arrived, the girls
went off to play. The boys had an idea.

It was the kind of idea that needed a big
hairy toy spider and a pair of pongy socks.

Then all they had to do was wait a while . . .

...until the girls got into
their sleeping bags...

...and then got out again very quickly!

"Aaaaaaaaah! A scary spider!" squealed little madam.

"Eeeeeeeew! A pongy sock!" cried cutie.

Little madam wasn't going to let the boys get away with that! She swung her pillow! "Take that!" she giggled.

"Oooomph!" puffed **little tinker**. "Careful!"
He gently lifted the secret bag out of the way
and sneaked his hand inside to flick a switch.
"What's in there?" demanded **little madam**.

They tried
asking nicely.

They tried turning
him upside down.

They tickled him
and squeezed him.

They tried everything, but **little tinker** just wouldn't tell! "It's a secret!" he said.

"I give up!" cried **little tough guy**. "Let's tell spooky stories!"

"...And then the giant monster ate them all up!"
Cutie finished off her story.
"Huh! That wasn't scary
at all!" laughed
little tough guy.

Just then, the friends heard a strange noise.
fizzzzzzzzzz

"Wh-wh-what's that noise?" asked
little sweetheart in a wobbly voice.
And there it was again.
fizzzzzzzzz... pop!

"Aaaaaaaah!" they screamed, diving for cover.

"I can hear it again – and I think I know where it's coming from!" said **cutie**, creeping around the room. **Little sweetheart** gasped.

fizzzzzzzzz....

pop!

"A-ha! It's coming from there!" cried **cutie**,
pointing to **little tinker's** bag with
the mysterious noisy thing inside.

"Make way!" cried **super hero boy**, leaping out of his sleeping bag. "I will save you!"

"Whoops," said **little tinker**.
"My secret is almost ready to eat!"
"Eat?" **little madam** wondered. What could it be?

"It's a popcorn maker!"
explained little tinker.

pop pop pop!
And sure enough, there was lots
and lots of yummy fresh popcorn!

As she watched, little sweetheart remembered
what every sleepover should have – the one thing
she had forgotten . . .

"A midnight feast!"
she cried, jumping up and down.

So that's exactly what they had.
"This popcorn is delicious!" munched
little tough guy, tucking into his third bowl.

"I'm so full up I'm going to **pop!**" giggled cutie.
Little sweetheart giggled too, and so did
all her friends. . .

Collect 5 tokens and get a free poster!*

All you have to do is collect five funky tokens!
You can snip one from any of these cool Bang on the Door books!

0 00 715313 9

0 00 715306 6

the cool sleepover secret

0 00 715297 3

0 00 715307 4

0 00 715308 2

0 00 715309 0

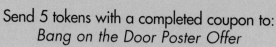

0 00 715312 0

0 00 715305 8

the groovy picnic surprise

Send 5 tokens with a completed coupon to:
Bang on the Door Poster Offer

PO Box 142, Horsham, RH13 5FJ
(UK residents)

c/- HarperCollins Publishers (NZ) Ltd,
PO Box 1, Auckland
(NZ residents)

c/- HarperCollins Publishers,
PO Box 321, Pymble NSW 2073, Australia
(Australian residents)

- ✂

Title: Mr ☐ Mrs ☐ Miss ☐ Ms ☐   First name: . . . .   Surname: . . . .

Address: . . . .

. . . .

. . . .

Postcode: . . . .   Child's date of birth: . . . . . . / . . . . . . /

email address: . . . .

Signature of parent/guardian: . . . .

Tick here if you do not wish to receive further information about children's books ☐

CS01

1 token

Terms and Conditions: Proof of sending cannot be considered proof of receipt. Not redeemable for cash.
Please allow 28 days delivery. Photocopied tokens not accepted. Offer open to UK and Australia and

the cool sleepover secret

When I was six and Peter was four, it changed.
There wasn't any laughing any more.
Dad was out all the time.
I'd come downstairs and find Mum crying.
She'd say, "Oh, I'm just tired"
but I knew it was more than that.

One night I suddenly woke up.
Mum and Dad were shouting and fighting.
I heard things falling on the floor.
Peter woke up too and we both started to cry.

After that Mum and Dad hardly spoke to each other.
It was horrible. I'd ask Dad if I could go to the park
and he'd say "Ask your mother".
I'd ask Mum for money for the school trip
and she'd say "Ask your father".

It was hard at school. I was thinking about
Mum and Dad and I couldn't pay attention.
My teacher asked what the matter was
but I didn't know what to say.
I just said "Nothing".

One day Dad just didn't come home.
He'd taken all his clothes and his records.
Mum said he'd left us.
It was a shock but somehow I wasn't surprised.
I'd known something was going to happen.
Mum said she and Dad were going to divorce.

I felt very scared. I had bad dreams.
I'd get up in the middle of the night
and get into Mum's bed where Dad used to sleep.
Peter started wetting the bed again
even though he was a big boy of four.
He was always whining and crying.

One day at school Gavin in my class
teased me about my picture.
I just went mad and started hitting him.
Miss had to stop me. Afterwards she was nice.
She said she knew about Dad going
and I could talk to her about it whenever I wanted.

I wanted Mum to explain why she and Dad
were going to divorce.
She said that they didn't get on any more
but they still loved me and Peter.

Whenever Mum started crying, I'd say
"Why don't you and Dad get together again
and we'll be a family like before?"
Mum said it wouldn't work.

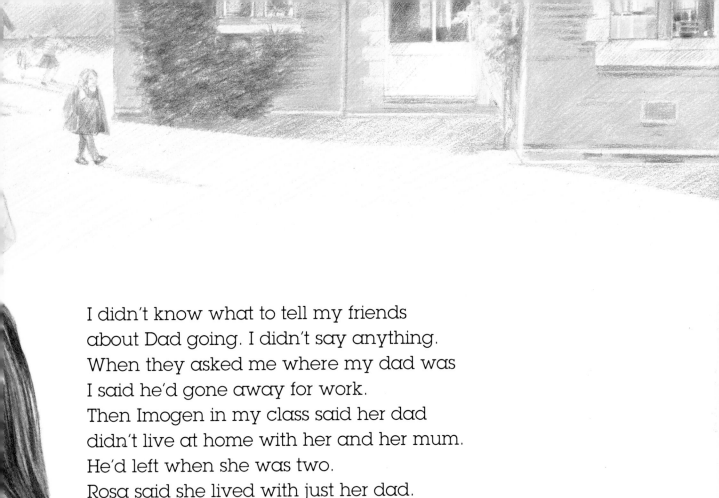

I didn't know what to tell my friends
about Dad going. I didn't say anything.
When they asked me where my dad was
I said he'd gone away for work.
Then Imogen in my class said her dad
didn't live at home with her and her mum.
He'd left when she was two.
Rosa said she lived with just her dad.
I was surprised that there were other children
whose parents didn't live together any more.

I thought that Dad might have left because
me and Peter had done something wrong.
Imogen and Rosa said it had nothing to do with the children
but with the mums and dads.

Mum and Dad couldn't agree
about who should look after us.
Mum said that Dad had gone to live with Stella
and it wasn't right for him to have us.
I didn't know what to say.
I wanted my dad as well as my mum.
It wasn't fair when other children have
their dad every day.

When Dad came to visit us, Peter would talk
like a baby and cry when Dad had to go.
I felt so sad, as though I was being split in two.

A court welfare officer came to talk to me.
She was friendly. She asked about school
and I told her about the swimming gala.
I said I loved my mum and I loved my dad
and so did Peter.

Now that it's sorted out, Peter and me
live with Mum and go to see Dad at weekends.
I can't have a cuddle with Dad every day any more
but it's all right. He talks to me a lot
and he's teaching me to ride my bike and write poems.

At first I didn't like to see him with Stella.
It didn't seem right. He should have been home with Mum.
I still find it strange that Dad's not at home.
Half of me seems to go one way and half the other.

After Dad went, Mum cried a lot and she was lonely.
Now she's much happier.
Peter and me went to see where she works
and we had tea in the office canteen!

Mum has a boyfriend now. She met him at work.
His name is Brian. At first I didn't like him.
I was afraid Mum wouldn't love me
and Peter any more. Also it made me realise
that Dad and Mum won't get back together again ever.

Now I'm glad Mum is happy with Brian.
I think he's nice. He doesn't pretend he's my dad.
He says he's a Step-Brian.

Once I thought Peter and me were the only children
in the world whose parents were divorced.
Now I know there are lots of children like us.
It's OK to love your mum and love your dad.
Even if they don't want to live with each other,
they are still your parents.

Now I know that when my parents divorced,
it wasn't because of me and Peter.
Parents can divorce but not children.
Even if they don't live together, your mum and dad
will always be your mum and dad.

Children Don't Divorce

by Rosemary Stones

Illustrated by Nicola Spoor

Published by Dinosaur Publications, an imprint of HarperCollins Publishers

When me and my brother were little
there was a lot of fun in our house.
My dad would tease me
and we would all play games together.
Mum and Dad would hold hands and hug each other.